Look Out
Kindergarten,
Here I Come!

by Nancy Carlson

PUFFIN BOOKS

PUFFIN BOOKS
Published by the Penguin Group
Penguin Putnam Books for Young Readers, 345 Hudson Street, New York, New York 10014, U.S.A.
Penguin Books Ltd, 27 Wrights Lane, London W8 5TZ, England
Penguin Books Australia Ltd, Ringwood, Victoria, Australia
Penguin Books Canada Ltd, 10 Alcorn Avenue, Toronto, Ontario, Canada M4V 3B2
Penguin Books (N.Z.) Ltd, 182-190 Wairau Road, Auckland 10, New Zealand

Penguin Books Ltd, Registered Offices: Harmondsworth, Middlesex, England

First published in the United States of America by Viking,
a division of Penguin Putnam Books for Young Readers, 1999
Published by Puffin Books, a division of Penguin Putnam Books for Young Readers, 2001

39 40

THE LIBRARY OF CONGRESS HAS CATALOGED THE VIKING EDITION AS FOLLOWS:
Carlson, Nancy L.
Look out, kindergarten, here I come! / Nancy Carlson.
p. cm.
Summary: Even though Henry is looking forward to going to kindergarten,
he is not sure about staying once he first gets there.
ISBN 0-670-88378-6
[1. Kindergarten—Fiction. 2. First day of school—Fiction.]
I. title.
PZ7.C21665Lim 1999 [E]—dc21 98-47039 CIP AC

Puffin Books ISBN 0-14-056838-7

Printed in the United States of America

To Maureen Beck—a dedicated educator who helped me come up with the idea for this book

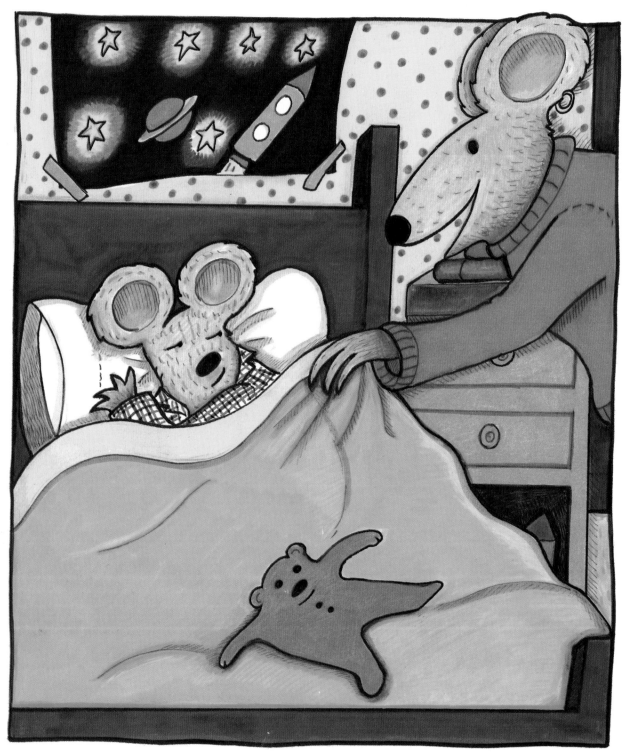

"Wake up, dear," said Henry's mom. "It's the first day of kindergarten."

"Oh boy! Let's go!" said Henry. He had been getting ready for this day all year.
"Not so fast," said his mom. "First you need to wash up and get dressed."

So Henry brushed his teeth the way his dentist had shown him and washed behind his ears.

Then he buttoned his shirt and snapped his jeans and *almost* tied his shoes.

"Okay, I'm all ready for kindergarten!" said Henry.
"Not so fast," said his mom. "First you need a
good breakfast."

So Henry ate three  pancakes and a bowl
of fruit and drank a big glass of milk.

"Now I'm ready to go!" said Henry.
"Not so fast," said his mom. "You still need to pack up your supplies."

So Henry packed pencils, scissors, crayons, paper, glue, an apple, and . . .

a photo of his mom and dad
(in case he got lonely).

"Now I'm ready!"
said Henry.

"What do you think we'll do first?" asked Henry.
"Do you think we'll paint?"

"Sure you will," said his mom. "Just like at home."
"Good!" said Henry. "What else will we do?"

"You'll probably learn your ABCs," said his mom.

"Hey, I already know the letters in my name!" said
Henry. "What will we do after that?"

"You'll sing songs,

and play games,

and you might practice counting," said his mom.

"One, two, three flowers," said Henry. "I can count to ten, because we practiced counting with buttons. What comes next?"

"You'll make fun things in arts and crafts, and you'll read stories."

"But I can't read!" said Henry.
"That's okay," said his mom. "You'll start by listening. Reading comes later."

"Here we are," said Henry's mom.
"It's so *big*," said Henry. "What if I get lost?"

"Remember, we found your room and your cubby at Kindergarten Roundup," said his mom. "But you can always ask a teacher for help."

When Henry got to his room and
saw lots of new faces, he said,

"I want to go home!"

"Why don't you come in and look around?" said his teacher, Ms. Bradley.

So Henry looked around. He saw the art corner.
He saw letters and numbers that he knew.

He saw a bookcase full of books, and he met a new friend to play with.

"Well, what do you think?" asked Henry's mom.
"I think I might stay for a while, Mom," said Henry,

"because kindergarten is going to be fun!"